SOMETHING
SPECIAL

Books by David McPhail

Henry Bear's Park
First Flight
Andrew's Bath
The Train
The Bear's Toothache
Something Special
The Party
Lost!

SOMETHING
SPECIAL

by David McPhail

Little, Brown and Company
Boston · Toronto · London

*The author wishes to thank John O'Connor
for his invaluable assistance*

*For Damon,
who is something special indeed*

Library of Congress Cataloging-in-Publication Data

McPhail, David M.
Something special / by David McPhail.
p.   cm.

Summary: Surrounded by parents and siblings with
remarkable talents, Sam yearns to be good at something
himself, and finds his own special niche when he discovers
the pleasures of painting.
ISBN: 0-316-56324-2
[1. Individuality—Fiction. 2. Artists—Fiction.
3. Family life—Fiction.] 1. Title.
PZ7. M2427So 1988.

[E]—dc19   88-2709
                                                        CIP
                                                        AC

Printed in the United States of America

Everyone in Sam's family could do something special.
Everyone but Sam.

Sam's sister Sarah played the piano.
Sam loved to watch her fingers fly over the keys.

But when Sam sat down to play it wasn't the same.
"You must have stone fingers, Sam!" Sarah cried.

Sam's sister Flo played first base.
She hardly ever missed a catch.

Sam could watch her play for hours.

Sam wanted to play baseball, too, but he couldn't catch a thing.

"Butterfingers!" said Flo.

Sam's brother, Eugene, was a computer whiz.
He really knew how to make that computer hum.

"Let me try," begged Sam.

But when Sam touched the computer it screamed!

And so did Eugene.

Sam's father was a wonderful cook.
Not only did everything taste good, it looked
beautiful, too.

Once Sam helped cook dinner, but no one was hungry.

Sam's mother carved wooden birds.
Sam thought they almost looked alive.
He wished he could carve birds, too, but he was
too young to use a sharp knife.

"Maybe Grandma will teach me to knit,"
thought Sam.
"She makes it look so easy."

But it wasn't.

The magician on T.V. made the disappearing
egg trick look easy, too.

But the trick didn't work for Sam, no matter how many times he tried it.

Even Sam's dog, Fred, could do something special.

"I can do *that!*" Sam said.

But he couldn't.

"What else can I try?" Sam wondered.
He walked down to the pond to see the ducks.
The birds were singing.

"Maybe I can sing!" he thought.
But not even the birds would listen.

Sam went to talk to his mother.
She was trying to paint a duck's feathers.
"I just can't get it right," she complained.

"Maybe it should be greener," said Sam,
"like the ducks in the pond."
"Show me," said Mother.

"Why, that's perfect!" Mother said.
"This is fun!" Sam said. "May I paint a picture?"

"That apple looks good enough to eat,"
said his father.

Next Sam painted a picture of Sarah with her flying fingers.

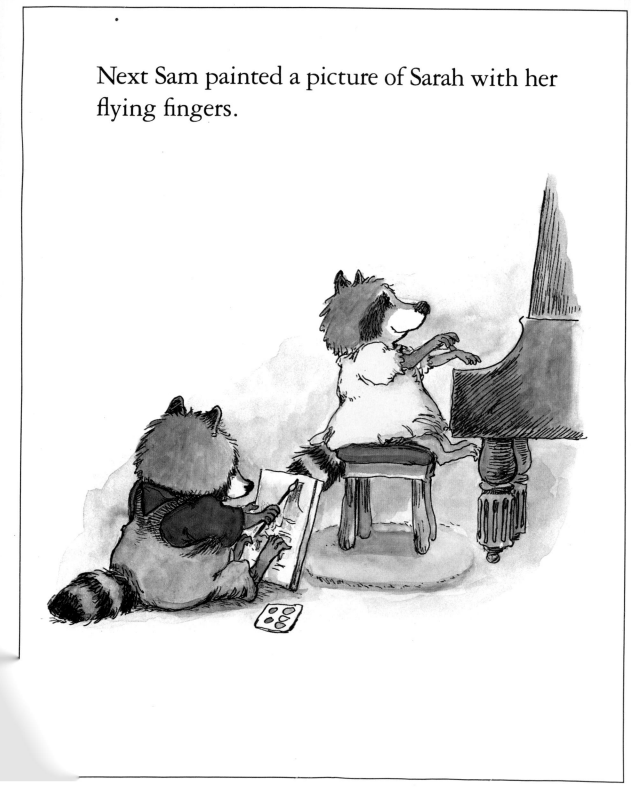

And one of Flo holding the trophy she'd just won.

"It looks just like you, Flo," said Sarah.

Then Sam painted a picture of Eugene and his computer with *all* its zips and zaps.

Sam's family thought that being able to paint
was something special . . .

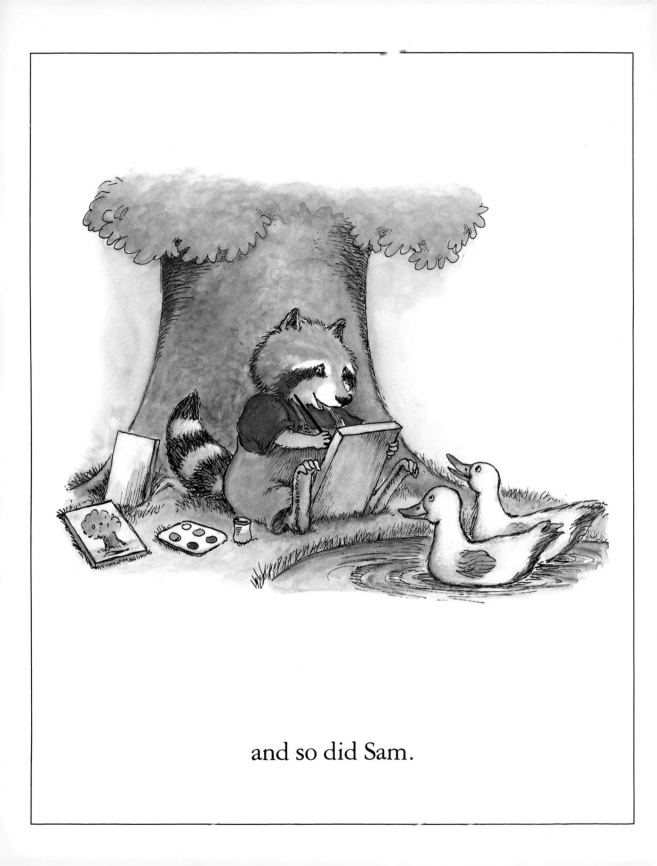

and so did Sam.